UNCLE BIGFOOT

BY GEORGE O'CONNOR

A NEAL PORTER BOOK
ROARING BROOK PRESS
NEW YORK

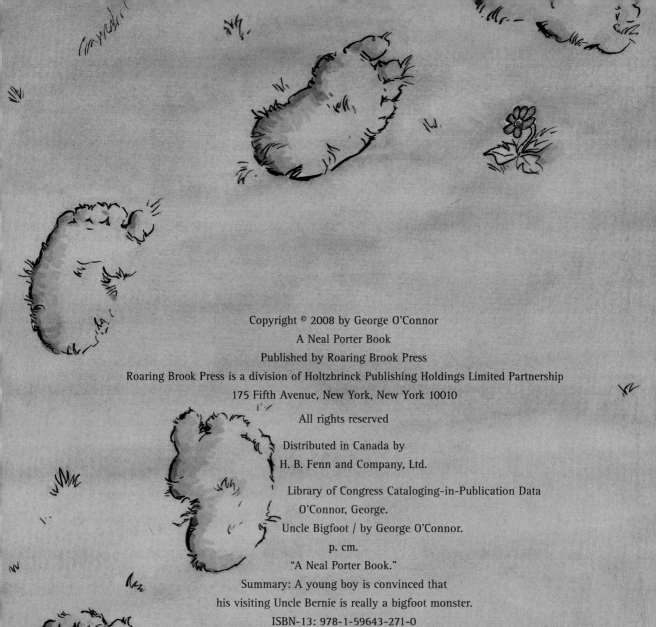

A Neal Porter Book

Published by Roaring Brook Press

Roaring Brook Press is a division of Holtzbrinck Publishing Holdings Limited Partnership

175 Fifth Avenue, New York, New York 10010

Distributed in Canada by
H. B. Fenn and Company, Ltd.

Library of Congress Cataloging-in-Publication Data

O'Connor, George.

Uncle Bigfoot / by George O'Connor.

p. cm.

"A Neal Porter Book."

Summary: A young boy is convinced that
his visiting Uncle Bernie is really a bigfoot monster.

ISBN-13: 978-1-59643-271-0

ISBN-10: 1-59643-271-3

[1. Uncles—Fiction. 2. Yeti—Fiction. 3. Family life—Fiction.] I. Title.

PZ7.O22185Unc 2008

[E]—dc22

2007009611

Roaring Brook Press books are available for special promotions and premiums.
For details, contact: Director of Special Markets, Holtzbrinck Publishers.

Printed in China

First Edition April 2008

2   4   6   8   10   9   7   5   3   1

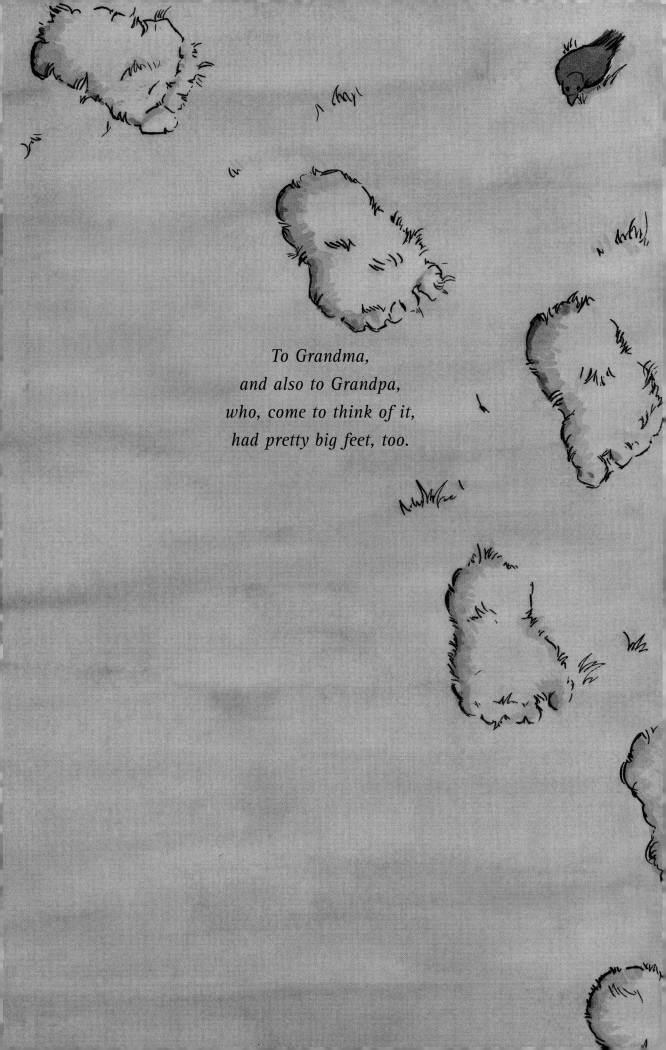

To Grandma,
and also to Grandpa,
who, come to think of it,
had pretty big feet, too.

"Oh, look, a postcard from your uncle Bernie,"
said Mom one day.
"He's coming to visit for a while."
"Uncle Bernie? Who's that?" I asked.

"I think you're too young to remember him," said Mom.

Uncle Bernie? I sure didn't remember any Uncle Bernie.

Later on, Dad and I got out the photo albums to see if we could find a picture of Uncle Bernie.

But *this* was the only picture we could find.

"Uncle Bernie's a little shy around cameras," said Dad.

Just who *was* this Uncle Bernie, and why didn't he like to have his picture taken? Did he have something to hide? What was his secret?

There were a lot of possible reasons.

One day there was a knock at the door.

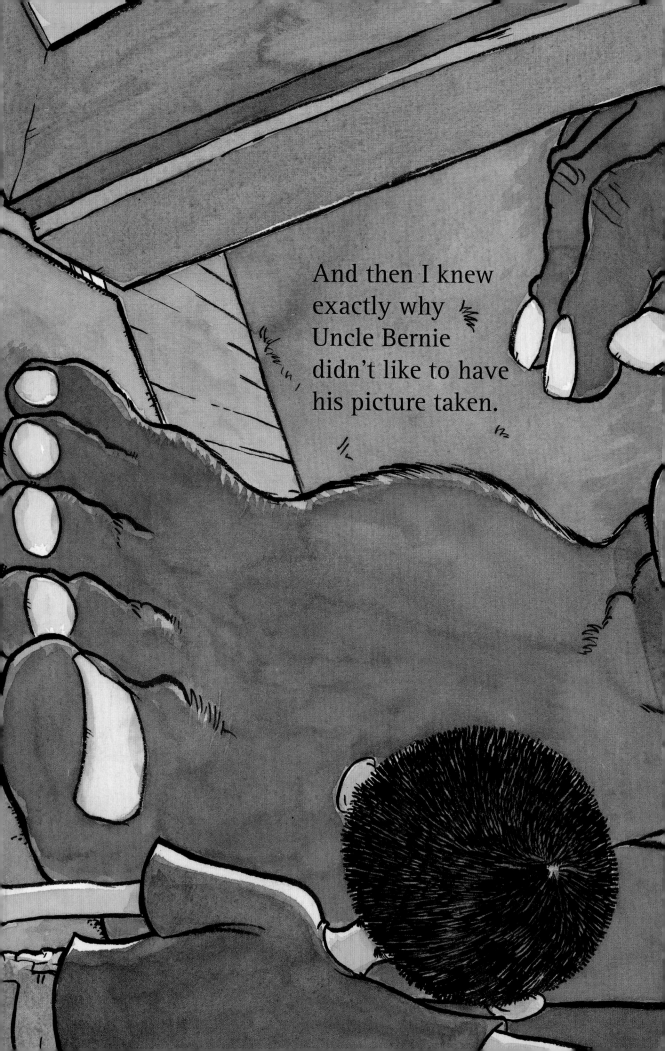

And then I knew
exactly why
Uncle Bernie
didn't like to have
his picture taken.

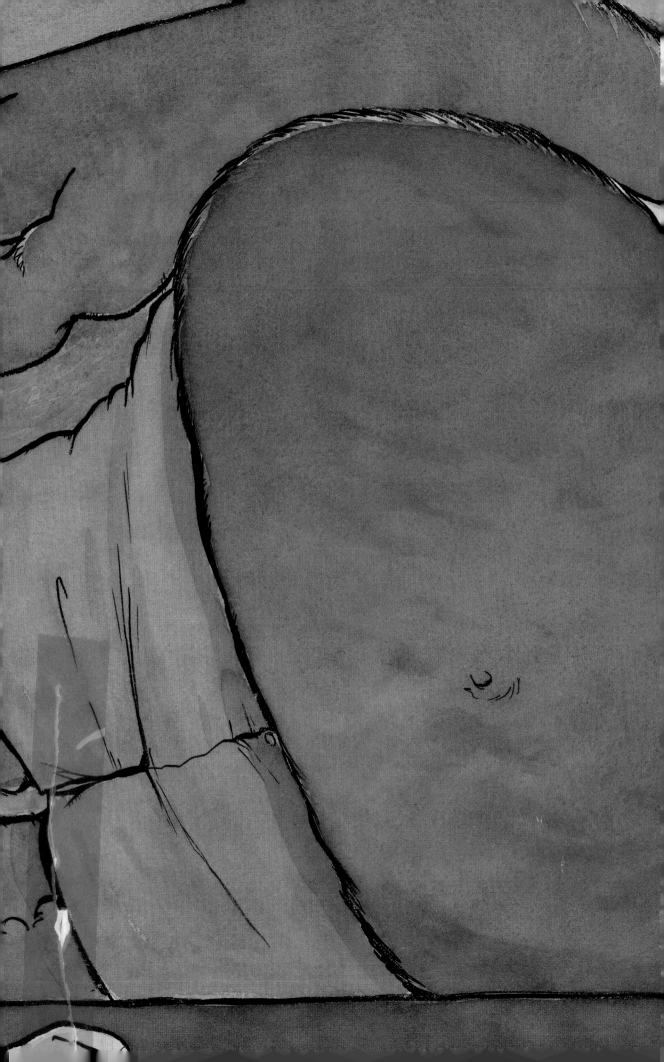

Bigfoots are big, hairy monsters that live far, far away in the deep, deep woods.

Nobody has ever taken a picture of one, but a few people have seen them.

VAMPIRES?

ALIENS?

SUPER VILLAIN

BIGFOOT

Luckily, my book had some drawings so I knew what to look for. First off, Bigfoots are supposed to be very hairy.

And Uncle Bernie has hair *everywhere*.

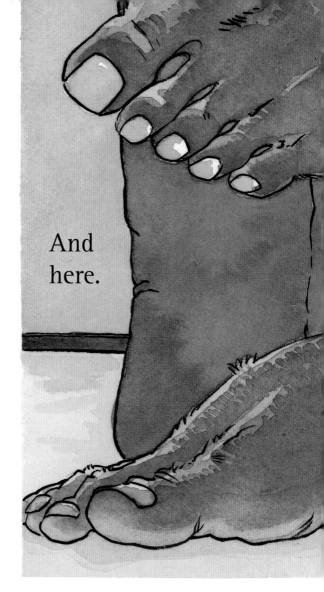

And here.

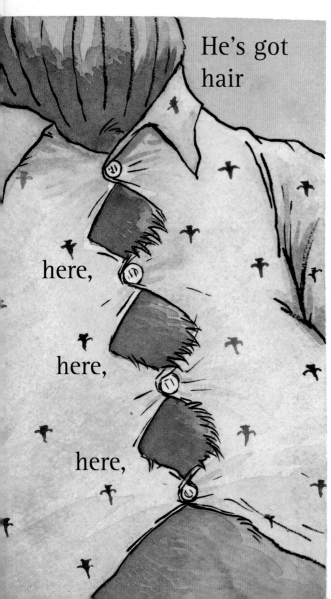

He's got hair

here,

here,

here,

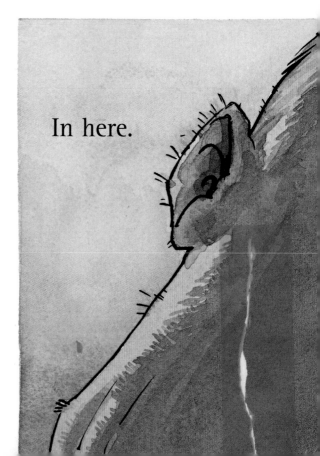

In here.

Here too.

There's some back there,

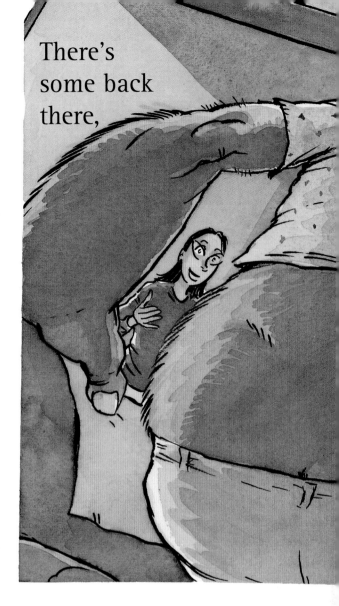

Not so much here.

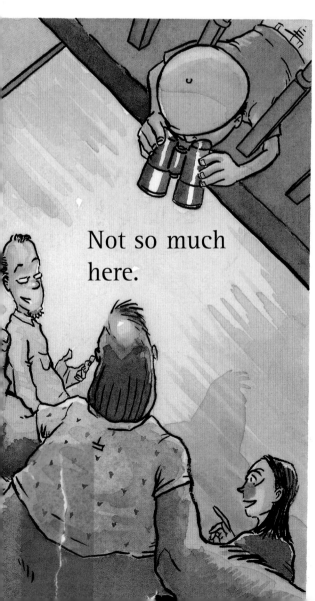

but all over here.

"What about his hair, Dad, huh? What about the hair?"

But Dad didn't think Uncle Bernie was a Bigfoot.
"Just wait until you get older, you'll be hairier too," said Dad.

Wait until I'm older?
What does that mean?

If my uncle is a Bigfoot,
what does that make me?!

Come to think of
it, Dad is pretty
furry too.

It's not just that Bigfoots are hairy, either.

My book says that Bigfoots have really big feet.

And Uncle Bernie has really, *really* big feet.

His feet
are sooo big
they should
be called . . .

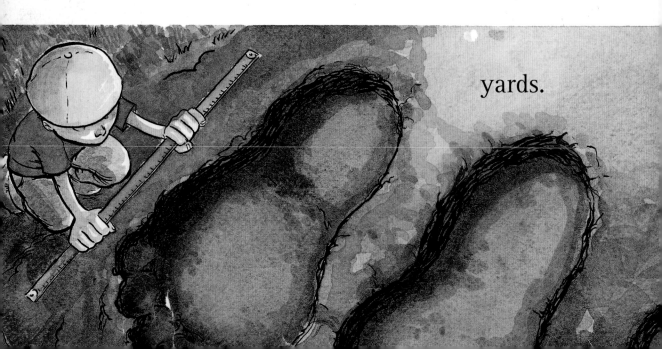

yards.

"What about his feet, Mom, huh? What about the feet?"

But Mom didn't think Uncle Bernie was a Bigfoot, either. "A lot of people have big feet. It doesn't mean that they're a Bigfoot," said Mom.

Mom had a point.
A lot of people do
have big feet.

But the book says a bunch of other things about Bigfoots.

Like Bigfoots have big hands.

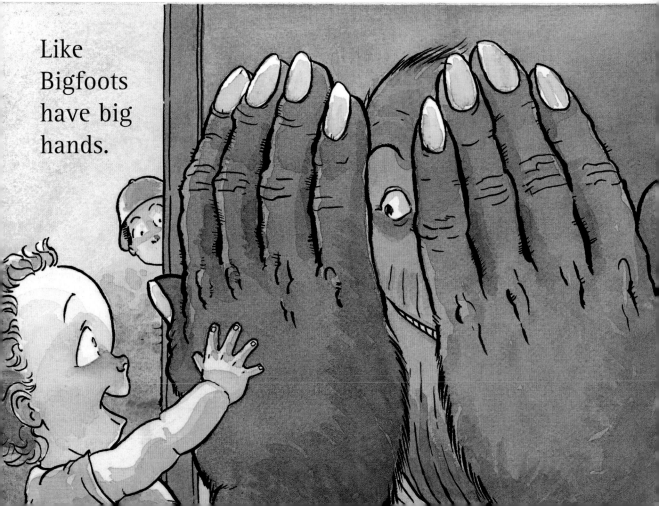

And Bigfoots have big muscles.

And Bigfoots have big appetites.

And big bellies.

Uncle Bernie has all those things too.

And the clothes he wears don't fit him right, like he just found them somewhere, and he never, ever wears shoes. . . .

But my book also says that Bigfoots are mean and scary. That doesn't sound like Uncle Bernie. He just seems a little . . .

different.

There are a lot of people
in the world and all of them
have something a little different
about them too.

Maybe some people are
just a little more different—

Like my Uncle Bigfoot.

Last Tuesday, Uncle Bernie had to go back home.
We all miss him, but I'm not too sad.

You see, we got
a postcard from
Scotland today. . . .

It says my
aunt Nessie
is coming
to visit.